SHAMGAR AND THE OX GOAD

115 Brocket Trail
Pocahontas, AR 72455

Shamgar and the Ox Goad

Untold Heroes of the Bible series: Volume One

capstoneproductions.org

Library of Congress Control Number: 2008911912

Ogden, Patti B.
Shamgar and the Ox Goad / by Patti B. Ogden
Illustrated by George Almond
Inspired by the sermons of William M. Branham

Summary: The story of one man and how he single-handedly delivered Israel
from the oppression of the Philistines.

Children's Religious Fiction

ISBN- 13: 978-0-9816783-7-5
Printed in the United States of America
First Edition

nd after him was Shamgar the son of Anath, which slew of the Philistines six hundred men with an ox goad: and he also delivered Israel.

Judges 3:31

Dedicated to today's battle-weary soldiers who hold God's standards high.

hamgar entered his barn with a sense of satisfaction. He and his family had worked hard all year. The Lord had blessed Shamgar with a plentiful harvest and he was well pleased with it. "Blessed be the Holy One of Israel, we'll have enough to feed the family this year," he thought. There had been too many nights of going to bed hungry, and Shamgar was determined that this winter would be different!

His mind raced over the past few years when the enemy had swooped in and

attacked the Israelite farms, terrorizing everyone in their path. Shamgar had

watched helplessly as the Philistines rode swiftly on horseback—pointing swords

and daggers—taking the little he had. Shamgar had no weapons and he was easily

outnumbered by the unrelenting soldiers. They had robbed all of his neighbors too.

Shamgar was incredibly angry about the way the Philistines were treating people.

Over the years, many mighty battles had been fought to conquer the oppressors.

Because Israel did not have a king or an army to fight against such attacks, every

man was on his own. Shamgar felt lack of unity was their shameful weakness and

the very reason the Philistines came and robbed them over and over again. They

had truly become a thorn in the flesh of Israel, just like the Bible said!

How Shamgar wished he could do something about it. He often daydreamed about solving the problem…but how? All of his time was spent doing farm work and taking care of his family. It was not possible for him to go away to be trained to become a mighty warrior.

His thoughts were interrupted as he heard a noise behind him. Turning quickly, he relaxed as he saw his wife coming towards him. Years of enemy attacks had made him nervous, and these days he jumped at anything out of the usual. His heart ached when he looked at his wife. She looked so pale. Her face was sunken from starvation and her elbows were poking out of the torn, ragged sleeves on her dress. Tears began to run down his cheeks as he tried to think of something cheerful to say.

"Well, wife dear, maybe this winter we won't starve if those Philistines will stay away. We can feed the children bread and barley as well. We can even have porridge for breakfast! I hope everything will be all right…honey, I am just so sorry," said Shamgar.

"It's all right, it's not your fault," she answered, trying to soothe his fears and guilt. "Your poor little arms look so thin, and your clothes are so worn. Maybe I can sell a little wheat and get some new clothes for you and the children…" said Shamgar, his voice weakened as he fought back his tears. She gave him a reassuring hug. "Yes dear, I know God will take care of us. He always does," she said kindly. They put their arms around one another in a comforting hug as they gazed upon a big bin of wheat.

Just then, Shamgar's little pale-faced children ran into the barn. The children loved to jump in a fresh pile of straw and smell its earthy scent on a brisk day. Such rollicking felt wonderful, especially after a full day of work on the farm. It almost made them forget the hunger pangs that haunted them for the past two years. Still in a playful mood, skinny little Samuel grabbed the ox goad and pretended it was a weapon, swinging it with all his might at the imaginary enemy.

The ox goad was a big stick about seven to ten feet long. On one end was a brass knob that was used to prod oxen. The other end was shaped into a useful tool to knock the dirt off a plow. Samuel was swinging it forcefully and it whipped through the air making a "whoosh" sound that thrilled his little brothers. "Samuel!" Mother cried, "Put that down! You'll hurt someone."

"But Mother, I was killing the bad old Philistines," he said as he laid the ox goad carefully against the grain bin.

"What a brave boy you are, Samuel," said Mother.

Surrounded by his beloved family, Shamgar was at peace again. This was always the case; whatever troubles were lurking about were quickly forgotten when Shamgar spent time with his wife and children.

"All is well," said Shamgar happily, "let's head into the house and get ready for dinner. Tonight we will celebrate our harvest and give thanks to Jehovah for all He has done for us."

Before leaving the barn, Shamgar and his wife decided to play a bit of hide-and-seek with the children. As they raced around the barn to find their hiding places, the children shrieked with glee. "Papa, come and find me," called one of the boys from the hay loft.

Tiny Rebekah climbed onto a window ledge, trying to get behind some dusty crates that the family used to transport small livestock from Jerusalem's old marketplace. Suddenly, she saw something outside the window.

"Oh, Mother, look there!" Rebekah warned, beginning to cry. Shamgar heard a familiar sound that sent shivers down his spine and stopped him in his tracks. His family—now silent and somber—froze with fear.

Tromp. Tromp. Tromp.

An army of nearly 600 Philistines, trained warriors from birth, were coming up the road! They were all in armor, carrying big spears, with swords hanging at their sides. Their helmets were thick, solid brass.

Tromp. Tromp. Tromp.

The men were marching up to Shamgar's farm to steal the fruit of his hard labor. "We are coming, Shamgar! You had a nice crop this year. We're glad you worked for us," taunted the leader of the Philistine army. Shamgar's wife began to cry, and the little children held on to one another as Shamgar peered out the window. Sure enough, those Philistines were on their way to rob them again!

The army was getting closer to the barn.

Tromp. Tromp. Tromp.

Shamgar began to pace back and forth. He didn't know what to do. He was a farmer, not a fighter. He didn't even have a sword, or a shield, or a helmet; but he knew what he did have: the promise of God!

Before he knew it, Shamgar began to feel a righteous indignation rise up within him. "I'm sick and tired of it! I'm not a warrior! I'm not a fighter! The odds are against me, and there's nothing I can do. Yet I know one thing...the Lord God of Israel is with me! That's all I know," shouted Shamgar.

Not wasting another moment, he grabbed the ox goad and leaped out of the barn.

"SHAMGAR!" screamed his wife, fainting.

The Philistines laughed to see Shamgar standing ready to fight. "Does he dare think he can whip 600 of us? What a puny man to try to show such bravery."

Shamgar stood his ground. "You come against me with man-made weapons, but I have something more powerful," he shouted above the ominous sound of swords being drawn from their scabbards. "I've had enough of you taking our food and invading our land!"

"Oh, yeah?" said the Philistine captain glaring at Shamgar with disgust. "And just what do you think you are going to do about it?"

"The Lord God said to Abraham that his seed shall possess the enemy's gates, and you are marching through my gate. You will not take what Jehovah gave to me. I come in the name of the Lord God of Israel!"

With that bold declaration of faith, Shamgar ran forward and began to swing the ox goad from side to side with full assurance in his heart that God would be in control of this battle.

The first swing he took blazed across a Philistine's head and killed him instantly, scattering his helmet into fifty pieces. He knocked the ox goad one way and then the other way until he overpowered every Philistine that dared jump in front of him. What a sight it was! A little man dressed in farm clothes conquering one enemy after the other under the supernatural power and force of God that drove him on and on until all 600 Philistines fell dead in front of him!

When that very last Philistine warrior fell in a heap before him, Shamgar raised his eyes toward heaven once more, but not in fear this time. He threw down the ox goad and cried, "Praise to Jehovah!" Tears of sweet relief flooded his eyes and ran down his stained face. He raised both of his hands in thanks to his merciful God for intervening at a time when Shamgar needed Him the most. No longer would the enemy take his family's food.

Shamgar's wife awoke just in time to hear his victory cry. She and the children ran and joyfully greeted their courageous protector, while giving all glory to Jehovah for such a miracle. Shamgar hugged his wife tightly. Scooping up his children, they all headed for the house.

Now it was really time for a celebration dinner!